THE MYSTERY AT

SHARK REEF

by Carole Marsh

Published by Gallopade International/Carole Marsh Books.
Printed in the United States of America.

First Edition ©2013 Carole Marsh/Gallopade International/Peachtree City, GA
Current Edition ©June 2016
Ebook edition ©2013
All rights reserved.
Manufactured in Peachtree City, GA.

Managing Editor: Janice Baker
Assistant Editor: Susan Walworth
Cover Design: John Hanson
Content Design: Randolyn Friedlander
Lighthouse photo p.95 courtesy of Bill Fitzpatrick (CC BY-SA 3.0)

Gallopade is proud to be a member and supporter of these educational organizations and associations:

American Booksellers Association
American Library Association
International Reading Association
National Association for Gifted Children
The National School Supply and Equipment Association
Museum Store Association
Association of Partners for Public Lands
Association of Booksellers for Children

Once upon a time …

> Hmm, kids keep asking me to write a mystery book. What shall I do?

Papa said …

> Why don't you set the stories in real locations?

You sure are characters, that's all I've got to say!

Yes, you are! And, of course, I choose you! But what should I write about?

 National Parks!

 SCARY PLACES!

 Famous Places!

FUN PLACES!

Disney World!

New York City!

Dracula's Castle

GRAND CANYON

 Write one about spiders!

We can go on the *Mystery Girl* airplane ...

I can FLY US anywhere!

Mystery Girl

Or aboard the *Mimi!*

Mimi

Take me to the Forbidden City!

Or by surfboard, rickshaw, motorbike, camel ...!

I can put a lot of **history, mystery, science,** legend, lore, and **laughs** in the books! It will be educational and fun!

Good stuff!

9

And so, join Mimi, Papa, Christina, Grant, Avery, Ella, Evan, and Sadie aboard the *Mystery Girl*—where the adventure is real and so are the characters!

START YOUR ADVENTURE TODAY!

www.carolemarshmysteries.com

A NEW SHARK SPECIES?

Maybe you think we have plenty enough sharks, but guess what? A new shark species has been discovered! The Carolina hammerhead was discovered off the South Carolina coast. Aren't I lucky—this is where I live...and swim!

In this story, you'll learn that sharks have a role in the natural world and we should be respectful of them. However, sharks are wild creatures and you should avoid swimming in the ocean at dawn and dusk when sharks may be feeding. Everything about sharks is fascinating, especially the story of prehistoric sharks that were as big as a school bus!

Join us on our new adventure—it's a mystery you can really sink your teeth into!

— *Carole Marsh*

1

SHARK TALE

Avery looked through the jaws of a shark large enough to swallow her. Although she was an athletic cheerleader and a good swimmer, she was thankful she was at the Palmetto Bluff Conservancy today and not swimming in the ocean.

She and her **mischievous**, blonde-haired brother Evan were visiting their grandparents, Mimi and Papa, at their new home in Palmetto Bluff, South Carolina, near the coast of the Atlantic Ocean. Since their grandparents had recently moved there, they'd been like kids exploring the area. "They call this part of South Carolina the 'Lowcountry,'" Papa had said in his deep, booming voice.

Avery and Evan had groaned when Mimi, a famous mystery writer, said she and Papa were taking them to hear a lecture. "Haven't we just gotten out of school?" Avery had whined.

"Yeah," Evan had agreed, "we're on vacation. We don't want to learn *anything*!"

Mimi had clamped her hands firmly over her short blonde hair to cover her ears. "You know I've got funny ears," she said. "There are some things they refuse to hear. Besides, if you don't like this lecture, I promise I'll play one of those silly video games that you know I'll lose."

Mimi was right again, Evan thought, once he learned the lecture was on sharks. His mouth was open wider than the shark jaws his sister held. *I love sharks!*

"Guess I won't be beating you at a video game," he whispered to his grandmother.

"These massive jaws belong to a great white," a pretty young woman named Melanie Garcia explained. "They are lined with hundreds of triangular teeth that are set in rows. As you can see, these **serrated** teeth are perfect for ripping the flesh off the shark's prey. They can tear off chunks of flesh that weigh 20 or 30 pounds. One of a shark's favorite foods is seal."

Thank goodness it's not girls, Avery thought as she held the powerful-looking jaws.

Mrs. Garcia, a **paleontologist** with the University of South Carolina, held up the shiny white tooth of a great white shark in one hand. Then she held up a brown, heart-shaped tooth larger than her other hand. "This is the fossilized tooth of a prehistoric shark called megalodon," she said. "Its name means 'giant tooth.' It swam in the world's oceans more than two million years ago."

"How about some more volunteers?" Mrs. Garcia asked, motioning for Mimi and Papa to join her at the front of the room. She opened a pair of cardboard jaws that had been propped against the wall and asked Mimi and Papa to step inside. The audience gasped.

"That shark could have swallowed Mimi and Papa in one gulp!" Evan exclaimed.

Avery giggled. She could just imagine Mimi walking around the inside of a shark in her favorite red high heels—she'd probably start decorating! And the cowboy hat that her tall Papa always wore would probably tickle the top of the shark's belly.

"The great white grows to an average length of 15 feet," Mrs. Garcia continued. "Megalodon grew to more than 50 feet. That's bigger than a school bus! In fact, it could have crushed a school bus in its jaws. It probably had the strongest bite of any animal that has ever lived. Its bite was even stronger than a Tyrannosaurus Rex dinosaur!"

"How do you know how long it was just by looking at its teeth?" Avery asked through the shark jaws.

"That's a great question!" Mrs. Garcia said. "We use a mathematical formula for that. We measure the length of one side of the tooth in inches and multiply it by ten. That gives us the approximate length of the shark in feet."

Evan was still impressed by the sight of his grandparents standing inside the massive jaws. "What did it eat?" he asked, hoping the answer wasn't grandparents.

"It's believed that the megalodons ate whales," Mrs. Garcia answered.

"Don't you have any real megalodon jaws?" another child asked.

"Shark skeletons are made of **cartilage**," Melanie explained. "That's like the stuff in your nose and ears."

Avery's face turned red. She had a feeling she knew what her silly brother was about to say. She had learned to expect it.

Evan snickered. "You mean boogers and wax?" he asked.

Mrs. Garcia laughed good-naturedly. "Guess I'll have to stop using that example," she said. "What I mean is that cartilage is very soft. It rarely fossilizes like bone. Finding an entire fossilized megalodon jaw would be very difficult. All that's usually found are the teeth."

"Where can you find **fossils**?" Avery asked, thinking she might start a new hobby.

"Believe it or not," Mrs. Garcia replied, "a man named Vitto Bertucci found one of the largest megalodon teeth ever discovered in a coastal riverbed right here in South Carolina! It was more than seven inches long. He was a jeweler who hunted fossils. It took Mr. Bertucci more than 20 years to find 182 teeth to place in a set of reconstructed megalodon jaws. They're 11 feet wide and nearly 9 feet tall. After he died, the set sold for more than $700,000!"

Everyone clapped after Mrs. Garcia thanked them for coming. "Before you leave, please take the time to look at all the fossils that are displayed," she added.

Evan and Avery made their way down the long tables filled with fossils. One tooth, tan and smooth, caused Evan to stop. He locked his hands and held them over the fossilized chomper. It was larger than both his hands put together. Near the top of the tooth he noticed a blackened area with a hole in it. "Guess this guy didn't floss," he said.

Evan hadn't seen Mrs. Garcia come up behind him. "You remind me of my son Noah," she said. "He thinks the same way that you do."

"Are these fossils valuable?" Avery asked Mrs. Garcia.

"They're all valuable," Mrs. Garcia said. "Some of them are priceless. But their value to me is not measured in money. It's measured in the stories they tell me about the past."

"What's your family doing for dinner tonight?" Mimi said, thinking that Avery and Evan might like to get to know someone their age who lived in the area. "We're taking Avery and Evan to one of our favorite cafés, Buffalo's. Maybe you could all join us."

"That sounds great," Mrs. Garcia said. "I'll call my husband to pick up Noah and meet us there. I just have to get all these fossils packed up first."

"Can we help?" Papa offered.

"Thanks," she said. "My assistant Sam will help. He's a graduate student in paleontology. He knows how to handle the fossils correctly."

Avery looked at the young man. He was thin with dark hair that fell to his shoulders and his clothes were rumpled, like he'd slept in them for days. He was talking to two men in the back of the room. While most of the people at the lecture had been parents and children dressed in casual shorts and flip-flops, these two men were wearing heavy boots. The boots were covered in a white dust that reminded Avery of baby powder. She watched Sam reach into his pocket before shaking hands with one of the men.

Avery had never even met Sam, but she had a strange feeling. Or maybe it was a hunch, like the characters in Mimi's mystery books often got when they met the bad guy.

There's something suspicious about this Sam character, she thought.

2

TUSK, TUSK

"Bwaaaaak, Bwaaaak, Bwaaaaaaaaak,"
Evan trumpeted across the screened porch
of the café as he clapped his arms together.
Sweet potato fries were stuck in each corner
or his mouth like tusks.

"Stop it, Evan!" Avery scolded. "People
are staring at us."

"I'm a walrus!" he said. "That's a type
of seal, and you sharks love seals!"

"I'm not a shark, Evan," she said. "I
was only holding the jaws!"

"I don't know," Evan said, shaking his
head as he continued to clap his arms like
flippers. "Your mouth is awfully big!"

"Ha, ha, ha," Avery said. "You're not
funny. Have you looked in the mirror lately?

With those big teeth you have, you're the megalodon mouth."

"OK, you two!" Mimi warned, as she dusted her large Caesar salad with black pepper. "I can tell you two are brother and sister!"

Avery looked at her little brother with a bit of a smile. Sure, he could be a pesky pain in the rear, but she loved him dearly. She knew this trip to South Carolina would be a lot of fun. The two had been looking forward to hanging out at Mimi and Papa's new home, where they got undivided grandparent attention!

"Mimi, you need to calm down with that pep..pep..pepper... *AAAACHOOOOOOOO!*" Evan exploded with a sneeze that launched one of the fries out of his mouth. It darted across the café like a rocket.

"Great aim!" a boy about Evan's age said as the fry pinged him in the middle of his forehead. "Playing walrus?" he asked knowingly. "These fries make the best tusks—nice and crisp so they hold their shape! It gives them great **velocity**!"

Avery was mortified. The boy was with Mrs. Garcia. He had brown hair and looked tall for his age. But his most distinguishing feature was the dimple in his chin.

"Sorry we're late," Mrs. Garcia apologized. "It took longer to load those fossils than I thought. This is my husband, Chris, and my son, Noah."

Avery figured that Noah must have gotten his height from his dad. She looked up at his face. He wasn't an old man, but his face looked weather-beaten, like he'd spent a lot of time in the sun.

Mr. Garcia shook hands with Mimi and Papa. After he ordered a pizza for Noah and his mom to share and two burgers for himself, Mr. Garcia confessed. "The truth is I made us late," he said. "But believe me, you didn't want me to come before I took a shower. I smelled too fishy."

"Are you a fisherman?" Papa asked as he forked some crab cake in his mouth.

"Something like that," Mr. Garcia said. "I'm a **marine biologist** with NOAA."

Evan looked at Noah with admiration. "You mean you're a marine biologist, too?" he asked the boy.

Mr. Garcia saw Evan's expression and grinned. "Not exactly! The government agency I work for sounds just like my son's name. You're not the first person who's been confused. NOAA is an acronym. The letters stand for something: National Oceanic and Atmospheric Administration."

"You're one of the weather people!" Mimi said.

"That's what most people think of when they think of NOAA," Mr. Garcia said. "But I work for the fisheries division. We work to protect marine wildlife. Right now, I'm leading a research project to study a new **species** of shark discovered off the South Carolina coast. It's been named 'Carolina hammerhead.'"

Avery's eyes grew wide. She'd never met a family with two scientists. "You must have studied STEM," she said.

Noah saw his dad's puzzled expression and explained. "That's an acronym too, Dad," he said. "We learned about it in school this year. It's all about the importance of Science, Technology, **Engineering**, and Math."

"Well, we didn't call it STEM when I was in school," Mr. Garcia said. "But I certainly use all those things every day in my job."

"So do I," Mrs. Garcia said. "We wouldn't know nearly as much about sharks—the ones we have today or the prehistoric ones—without each of those STEM tools."

Avery stared out at the sky. It was turning dusty pink and the sinking sun changed the blue May River into liquid gold as it calmly flowed past the café. She thought about what Mrs. Garcia had told them about the megalodon teeth found in South Carolina and wondered what ancient fossils might be sleeping in the riverbed nearby.

"Do you think we could find any megalodon teeth around the May River?" Avery asked Mrs. Garcia.

"Hmmm," Mrs. Garcia replied, thinking a moment. "Tell you what—I'd like to challenge the three of you to use your STEM skills to answer that question for yourself."

"That's a great idea!" Mimi said. She was always ready to jump on the bandwagon of anything educational. "After you do all the research and figure out the best place to look, you could engineer the tools you'll need. When you're ready, Papa and I can take you on a fossil-finding **expedition!**"

Avery, Evan, and Noah exchanged excited glances. Outside, a gust of wind stirred the palmetto trees. They shook their feathery tops like cheerleaders shaking their pompoms.

This is not going to be just another summer vacation, Avery thought. *This is going to be an adventure!* Little did she know that adventure would soon take a sharp turn.

When they had all finished their homemade ice cream, they walked together to the parking area. Avery and Evan were climbing into Papa's big, black SUV when Mrs. Garcia screamed. The fossil collection had disappeared from her van!

3

A CURIOUS CLUE

"I came right from The Conservancy," Mrs. Garcia said. She was near tears. "I'm sure I locked the van. In fact, I had to unlock it to get in!"

Everyone looked in the back of the van and saw it was empty. Even the foam padding that had been between the boxes to protect them was gone.

Mr. Garcia dialed the police. Noah hugged his mom. He knew how much the fossils meant to her and her work.

Avery, who had recently become interested in sleuthing, thought of Sam and the conversation he'd been having with the men who looked out of place.

"Maybe you should call your assistant, Sam," Avery suggested. "Maybe he took them out and forgot to tell you."

"Sam would never take the fossils without telling me," Mrs. Garcia insisted.

Avery was **skeptical**, but kept her suspicions to herself. She looked at her phone. They'd been in the restaurant for more than an hour—plenty of time for someone to break into the van. Why hadn't anyone seen something? But then she noticed that Mrs. Garcia had parked at the end of the parking lot right beside Papa's SUV. It was large enough to block the van from the sight of do-gooders who might report a crime.

What are the ways someone could get into a locked van? she thought. *They could break a window, but the window wasn't broken. They could cut a hole in floor of the van, but it would be difficult to get the large boxes out that way, and someone would definitely notice that. They could cut a hole in the roof of the van. Hmmmm, better double-check that one.*

"Hey, Evan!" Avery called. "Come here a second!" She made a stirrup with her hands.

"See if you see anything strange on top," she instructed him. Evan clung to the side of the van like a tree frog as Avery slowly lifted him high enough to see over the top.

"Just needs a good scrubbing!" Evan said as Avery lowered him to the ground.

Avery thought some more. *They could pick the lock, or...of course!* She hadn't thought of the easiest way to get into the van—*a key! Could that be what Sam had pulled out of his pocket to give the men?*

Before Avery could ask Mrs. Garcia if Sam had a key to the van, two police cars pulled into the parking lot. Their red and blue lights were flashing brightly, but there were no blaring sirens.

One of the officers pulled out a kit and started dusting for fingerprints. "I'd better tell him you touched the van," Avery told Evan. "I wouldn't want them hauling you off to jail."

Another officer was filling out a report. Avery heard him ask Mrs. Garcia the value of the stolen merchandise. She answered, "Priceless!"

"I guess that's why someone would want to steal them," Evan said, as he recalled the story about the giant megalodon jaws. "They can sell them for a fortune."

Noah joined Avery and Evan who were leaning on the front of Papa's SUV. "Looks like this is gonna take a while," he said. "We might as well go and sit down at one of the tables out front."

"Noah," Avery asked, "what do you know about Sam?"

"Are you talking about my mom's assistant?" he asked.

"Yes," she replied.

"Not much," he said. "He came over to our house for dinner one night, but he didn't talk too much. At least, not until he and mom started talking about fossils."

Crossing the parking lot, Avery stepped on something that she felt through the sole of her purple sneaker. She stopped and looked under her foot. It was a blob of dried mud, but it wasn't the regular brown kind. This mud looked chalky white. "That's weird," Avery said as she scraped her shoe on the curb.

"You coming?" Evan asked when he noticed that Avery had fallen behind.

But something else had stolen Avery's attention—a piece of paper flapping in the gentle breeze. At first, she figured it was trash, probably the wrapper from a hamburger that had blown up against the base of the tree. But then she remembered what her cousin Christina had told her.

Christina had traveled the world with Mimi and Papa and each trip had usually found her tangled up in some sort of mystery. It seemed to run in the family. Christina had said that clues could turn up in the strangest ways and in the strangest places.

Avery picked up the paper. If it wasn't important, she still needed to throw it in the trash. She had learned that every piece of trash can have an impact. It could blow into the river, wash out to sea and eventually kill a marine animal that might be on the endangered species list.

The scrap of paper had definitely been around a hamburger. But there was writing on the inside, as well as grease dots and bits of dried cheese. She showed it to Noah and Evan.

"It looks like some sort of graph!" Avery said.

Noah looked at the paper. "I think it's a timeline," he said.

Written below the timeline were the words:

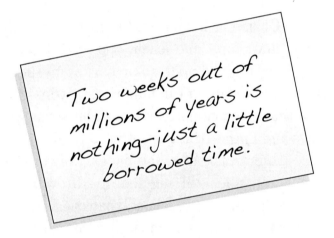

Two weeks out of millions of years is nothing—just a little borrowed time.

4

FLOATING FISH GUTS

Evan watched the fish guts rise and fall on the foamy water. The boat rocked under his feet. He wiped his face as a cold sweat broke out all over his body.

"Noah," he whispered. "I think I'm going to be—" Evan hung his head over the ship's rail and lost his lunch.

Avery ran to the galley.

"Don't be embarrassed," Noah said, when Avery returned with a cold, wet cloth. "I got sick the first few times I came out, too."

"Really?" Evan asked.

"Sure," Noah replied. Leaning close to Evan's ear, he whispered. "I still get queasy sometimes, especially right after I've eaten."

Evan was relieved to know that someone named after the man who built the Ark in the Bible got seasick too.

"I guess I should have eaten salad instead of that greasy grilled cheese," Evan said. "I'll know better next time. At least, if there is a next time."

"I'm sure you'll have another chance before you go back home," Noah said.

Mr. Garcia had invited the kids to come along on his small research vessel, *The Worm*, while he attempted to tag the newly-identified Carolina hammerhead he'd told them about the night before. For Evan, who had only seen live sharks at the Georgia Aquarium in Atlanta, this was a big deal.

Avery was still fretting about the missing fossils and the mysterious note they'd found, but that would have to wait for a while. How often did a kid get to snag a ride on a real research ship? Like Evan, she thought sharks were interesting. But getting close enough to put a tag on one was maybe a little too close?

"No worries," Noah told her. "My dad puts the tags on. You'll be completely safe. I've watched him do it lots of times."

"Do you want to be a scientist when you grow up?" Avery asked. "It seems like a family tradition."

Noah smiled. "I haven't decided yet," he said. "I've been thinking a lot about space exploration. I mean, how cool would it be to help set up a colony on the moon?"

Evan nodded in agreement. The sickly green tint he'd felt before his eyes was slowly fading to its normal hue. "That would be awesome!" he said. "Think you could invite me to tag along on that trip too?"

"Sure," Noah said. "As long as you promise not to eat a grilled cheese before we launch."

"Deal!" Evan said, shaking Noah's hand to seal the promise. "I promise not to launch my lunch!"

The ship's bell sounded. *CLANG! CLANG! CLANG!*

"What does that mean?" Evan asked.

"They must have spotted something," Noah replied.

They felt the ship surge beneath their feet as the water began to churn around them. "They've fired up the engine," Noah said. "Hang on!"

The research vessel was no longer bobbing in the water like a cork. It was flying! The wind blew Evan's blonde hair off his face. It felt even more refreshing than the wet washcloth, and he felt a renewed sense of adventure.

"Look at that!" Avery shouted gleefully as she pointed at three dolphins. They seemed to share the kids' excitement as they skimmed through water beside the boat like sleek jet skis.

Noah grinned at Evan, stood up, and held his hands in front of him like they were rocket ships.

Mr. Garcia flopped out of the cabin like an overgrown frog in his wetsuit and flippers. Another man followed him holding a wire about the length of a pencil. A small object, not much larger than an eraser, bobbed on the end.

"You kids having fun?" the man said cheerfully. "I'll let you ride in the cabin on the way in to Hilton Head," he said. "Maybe even make some radio calls!"

"Who's that?" Evan asked.

"That's Jack," Noah said. "He works on all the electronic equipment they use to track the sharks. My dad says he's an electronic genius."

"Seems like a nice man," Avery said.

Mr. Garcia and Jack joined several other men at the stern. Noah had informed Evan never to call it "the back of the boat."

After Mr. Garcia pulled on a mask, he stuck a snorkel in his mouth. The boat slowed, then stopped. He was staring into the deep water and pointing excitedly. His assistant tied a humongous fish head to a piece of rope and dropped it into the water with a splash.

Avery was horrified when Mr. Garcia picked up a long stick with a sharp pointed end as Jack hooked the wire to it. It looked like a spear. "I thought your dad was studying sharks, not killing them!" she shouted at Noah.

"Don't worry, Avery," Noah said. "They're not hurting the sharks. That's how they put the tags in their fins." He pointed at the tiny diamond earrings sparkling through her shoulder-length, strawberry-blond hair. "Dad said it's like getting a pierced ear. Their fins are made of cartilage and they don't even bleed. C'mon, let's go and watch."

Evan approached the stern cautiously with Avery beside him. At least they weren't using the floating fish guts to attract sharks this time. They peered into the seemingly bottomless water of the Atlantic Ocean and gripped the ship's rail so tightly their knuckles turned white. What they saw made them gasp. *Could it possibly be real?*

5

ALIEN HEAD

Mr. Garcia plunged into the water right beside the strangest beast Evan and Avery had ever seen. It belonged in a science fiction comic book, not the ocean! Its body, which was about 10 feet long, looked like a shark, but the head was out of this world! The alien-looking noggin stuck out on either side almost like wings, wide and flat. Most bizarre of all were the eyes. One stared to the left and one to the right on the very end of each "wing."

"It's a hammerhead all right!" Noah exclaimed.

Of course Evan had seen pictures of hammerhead sharks before, but nothing could have prepared him for seeing one in the wild. "Its head doesn't look much like a hammer to me," Evan said, as he watched the shark circle Mr. Garcia. "It looks more like a wide shovel, or the capital letter T, or kind of like the spoiler on a race car."

"Or maybe that wide thing on the end of a vacuum cleaner," Avery said, struggling to find words to describe the fish's freaky face.

"You're right," Noah agreed with them. "Let's just hope it's the right kind of hammerhead."

"What do you mean?" Evan asked. "Isn't the new species called the 'Carolina hammerhead,' and aren't we off the coast of South Carolina?"

"Yeah," Noah said. "But there are about nine different species of hammerheads. The new species looks a lot like the scalloped hammerhead. It's hard to tell them apart."

"What's the difference?" Evan asked.

"My dad said the Carolina hammerhead has fewer vertebrae than the scalloped hammerhead," Noah explained. He reached back to touch his spine. "You know, the bones down their backs."

Suddenly, the hammerhead rolled to the side and snatched the fish head off the rope. Evan and Avery got a good look at its rows of jagged teeth. As it swam away, Mr. Garcia aimed and stuck the end of the sharp stick into the fish's top fin.

"Got him!" cried Noah, slapping Evan a high five. "Right in the dorsal fin!"

"Don't you worry that your dad will get bitten?" Avery asked Noah.

"Sure I do," Noah said. "Sharks are dangerous. But hammerheads very rarely attack humans. They mostly eat fish and squid. Besides, my dad has been studying them a long time and he's careful. I would never get in the water with one, though!"

Evan expected Mr. Garcia to be happy when he climbed back on the ship. Instead, he looked disappointed. Avery wondered if he was worried about Mrs. Garcia and the missing fossils. She always thought scientists' lives would be all about adventure and discovery, but these two seemed to have a lot to worry about.

"Let's take it in, guys," Mr. Garcia said to his crew. "Half a day on the water and only one shark." He followed Jack back into the cabin. "Let's see if this tag is working correctly."

"What's he talking about?" Evan asked.

"They've been having trouble tracking the sharks they've tagged," Noah explained. "It's like they'll pick up their signal for a while, and then they just disappear."

There's that word again, Avery thought. *Why are so many things disappearing around here?*

The hammerhead shark's wide-set eyes help it scan the deep ocean for prey!

6

FISH SANDWICH

The kids followed Jack and Mr. Garcia into the cabin. Monitors and lights flashed and blipped all around them.

"This looks more like a spacecraft than a ship," Evan said, admiring all the gadgets.

"Shhh," Avery said. She grabbed Evan's shoulders and pulled him back. "If we're not quiet, they might make us get out."

The three kids sat on a bench in the back of the cabin as the men **persistently** pressed buttons and adjusted dials. The light from the computer screens cast an eerie glow in the cabin and for a minute, Avery forgot that she was at sea.

"If any of you kids have a cell phone or electronic game, please make sure it's turned off," Mr. Garcia said. "This equipment is very sensitive, and those things might cause interference."

"There he is!" Mr. Garcia exclaimed. A tiny blip bounced across the screen. "I don't understand it," he added. "Every time we tag a shark, the equipment seems to be working fine. Then, the next time we try to locate the shark, it has stopped working."

Jack patted Mr. Garcia on the back. "Don't worry, boss," he said. "I'm sure we'll get it figured out."

"I wish I could be as carefree as you, Jack," Mr. Garcia said. "Unfortunately, I could lose my job if this problem isn't corrected."

Avery looked at Noah. Deep lines were forming between his brows. Avery knew what he was thinking: *both* his parents could be in danger of losing their jobs!

Mr. Garcia headed for the cabin door and ruffled Noah's coal-black hair as he passed by. "I'm going to my office to fill out some reports," he said. "You kids stay out of trouble, and no swimming with the sharks!"

Evan looked concerned. "He's got to be joking, right?"

Avery and Noah laughed. "You know," Avery said, looking at her brother, "you're just about the right size to make a good filet of fish sandwich for some hungry shark!"

"Yes," Noah agreed. "All you would need is an order of fries to go with you!"

"Not funny!" Evan said. He wrapped his arms around his body like he was giving himself a big hug to stop a shudder. "Didn't you see what that hammerhead did to that fish head?"

"Stop picking on him!" Jack said. "No kid on this ship will be fish food as long as I'm around!"

Jack smiled at Evan and patted a tall stool beside him. "How'd you like to use the radio?" he asked. "You can let the station know we're heading in."

"Awesome!" Evan said. He clamped headphones over his ears that made him look like some kind of bug. "This is *The Worm*—heading to port," he said very officially.

"See?" Jack said. "Isn't this better than being a fish sandwich?"

Evan grinned broadly as he continued listening to the radio chatter in the headphones.

Jack crossed the cabin to adjust some equipment. Avery, who was watching the shark blip, tapped Noah and pointed at the screen. *It had suddenly gone blank!*

7

PUPS

The kids stood at the front rail of *The Worm* as the ship's bow aimed for the dock. "That looks like a giant candy cane!" Avery said, pointing to a tall, red-and-white striped object in the distance.

"That's the Harbour Town Lighthouse," Noah explained. "It's the best-known lighthouse around here, but it's not terribly old. It was built in the late 1960s."

"Is there an older one?" Avery asked. Really old things always fascinated her.

"Yes," Noah said. "It's called the Hilton Head Rear Range Light, but you can't see it from here. It's on the other side of the island. It's not nearly as pretty as Harbour Town Lighthouse, but it was built in the

1800s. And..." he added, dropping his voice to a creepy whisper, "it has a ghost!"

"Maybe I can get Mimi and Papa to take us there!" Avery said. "I love ghost stories!"

"Better hold on to the rail," Noah warned as the ship bumped against the old tires tied to the dock to cushion the impact.

As soon as the ship was securely docked, the kids climbed onto the gangplank that led to the pier.

"OOOOH!" Evan said, wobbling left and right. "My legs feel like Jell-O!"

Noah laughed at his new friend. "You're still walking on your sea legs," he explained. "It will take a little while for you to get your land legs back."

Evan looked down at his skinny tanned legs sticking out from under his khaki shorts. "They look like the same legs I've always had," he said.

"They are the same, silly," Avery said. "It's just that when you're on a ship, your balance has to get used to the rocking motions of the sea. Then, when you get back on the land, which isn't moving around like the sea, your legs feel weird and your balance is off."

"OK," Evan said. "But I still think it feels like Jell-O legs. And speaking of Jell-O, I could sure go for something to eat."

"C'mon," Noah said, heading into the NOAA station. "I know where my dad hides his stash of snacks."

Mr. Garcia walked in as the kids were tearing like sharks into a package of peanut butter crackers. "As soon as you're finished," he said, "why don't you go feed the pups? The food is already measured out in the refrigerator."

"Pups!" Avery shouted. She'd had enough sea creatures for one day and was excited to see something soft and furry.

"You may be surprised when you see these pups," Noah said. "They don't even bark." He led them to a back room where Avery could hear the sound of humming motors and the gurgle of water.

"It sounds like my aquarium back here," Evan said.

Noah opened an old refrigerator and pulled out a plastic bag.

"Yuck!" Avery said when she saw that the bag contained little fish. "Who feeds that to puppies?"

"But it's what they like," Noah said with a sly smile.

"Our dog—his name is Clue—would never go for that," Evan said, turning up his nose as Noah opened the bag. "That reeks!"

Noah took the fish to a shallow concrete tank with wide, thick sides and sat down. "Just watch how they go for it," he said, dropping a couple of the fish into the water.

Avery was amazed to see more than a dozen baby hammerhead sharks swimming toward the fish. "But where are the pups?" she asked.

"These *are* pups," Noah said. "That's what you call baby sharks."

"Well, I guess they are kinda cute," Avery commented, even though she was still disappointed they didn't have fur.

"Can I feed them?" Evan asked.

"Sure," Noah said. "Just don't put your fingers in the water. They may be cute, but they can still bite."

Evan plopped a few fish in the water. "They may not have fur," he said, intently watching the feeding frenzy, "but they would make great watchdogs. Nobody would want to tangle with those teeth!"

"You'd have to dig a moat around your house for them to swim in," Avery said, imagining the little sharks terrorizing would-be burglars. Then she asked, "Did they hatch out of eggs?"

"No, they didn't," Noah answered. "Baby hammerheads are born alive just like human babies. But there are some kinds of shark babies that come from eggs."

"Do you think they miss their mom?" Evan asked.

"Shark moms try to find a safe place to give birth so that nothing will eat their babies," Noah explained. "But once they're born, she just swims away. They're on their own."

"Did your dad catch them in the ocean?" Avery asked.

"Their mom was one of the Carolina hammerheads brought here for study," Noah said. "After she was in the tank, she had babies. Dad was so excited that he gave out candy bars to all the staff, and me, too!"

Avery's phone buzzed in her pocket. "Hi, Papa!" she said. "Yes, it was amazing. I can't wait to tell you all about it. Yes, he did, but he feels fine now. OK, we'll be waiting."

Avery ended the call. "Why'd you have to tell him I got seasick?" Evan grumbled.

"Because he asked!" Avery said. "He'll pick us up in a few minutes. He said he was in a hurry—something about a deal he had to make. I told him we'd wait outside."

Outside, Jack waved goodbye as he got into his truck. It was as red as Mimi's favorite shade of lipstick. He was carrying a small monitor similar to the ones in the boat.

"He's a nice guy," Evan said. "But his truck sure could use a wash."

"Yeah," Avery agreed. "There must be a lot of that white mud near his house."

Avery looked back at the boat. The sun reflecting on the water made her squint. She saw someone standing on the pier talking to one of the crewmen. He had rumpled clothes and dark hair. *She wasn't sure, but he looked an awful lot like Mrs. Garcia's assistant, Sam.*

Avery and Evan using their iPad for
shark research!

8
AVERY'S CLASSROOM

Mimi peeked out of her elegant laundry room where she did a lot of writing on her mystery books, but seldom any laundry. "How's it going?" she asked the kids who were gathered around Evan's iPad like sharks surrounding a wounded fish.

"Just doing some research on fossils," Evan said. "We're using our technology, Mimi. It's something you wouldn't understand."

Mimi laughed. "You're right, Evan. When I think of research, I still think about the encyclopedias in the library."

Since Noah's parents were working overtime to solve the problems they each had, Mimi had invited him to spend a few days with

Avery and Evan at her house. The kids were concerned about what had happened to Mrs. Garcia's fossils as well as what was happening with the sharks. But they hadn't forgotten their challenge to use STEM to find some fossils of their own.

"Maybe we can find enough fossils to replace the ones stolen from your mom," Evan suggested.

"Wouldn't that be awesome," Noah said. "We'd be on all the news shows, and our teachers would think we're so smart we wouldn't have to go back to school. I could get busy designing the rocket I'll need to take me to the moon!"

"Whoa!" Avery cautioned the boys. "One thing at a time. I think we'll be very lucky to find just one fossil."

Avery still hadn't decided what she wanted to do when she grew up, but today she was in the mood to be a teacher. She had set up a dry-erase board in the laundry room. Next, she pulled the hair band off her wrist and tugged her hair back into a ponytail like she meant business.

"Now," she said. "Let's go over what we've learned and write our plan."

The green marker squeaked across the board as Avery wrote.

"The coastal areas are a good place to look for fossils," Noah said. "And we're in a coastal area."

"One website said that it's good to look around streams and riverbeds," Evan said.

"And why is that?" Avery asked.

Evan tried to explain. "The water has cut through the cemetery rocks right down to the buried bones."

Noah giggled while Avery corrected her little brother. "It's **sedimentary rock**, Evan. The *cemetery* is where you bury dead people."

"Well," Evan said, shrugging his shoulders, "there are lots of bones in both places!"

"I also read that there are lots of fossils in **limestone** quarries in South Carolina," Noah said. "Maybe we could go to one of those."

"What's a limestone quarter?" Evan asked. "I thought quarters were made out of silver."

"My brother sometimes gets words confused," Avery explained to Noah. "He said *quarries*, Evan. That's where they dig limestone out of the earth. They use it to make things like fertilizer and cement."

"I'm not sure if there's a **quarry** close to here," Noah said. "I think we should stick with looking around the May River."

Avery and Evan were about to agree when Papa blew through the back door like a Texas tornado. The kids had never seen him so excited. "Guess what?!" he shouted.

"Did the police find the missing fossils?" Noah asked hopefully.

"No, I'm afraid that isn't it," Papa said. "Sorry!"

"Have they found a living megalodon?" Evan asked.

"No," said Papa, shaking his head back and forth so hard his Stetson cowboy hat twirled. "But my surprise is almost that big!"

9

PAPA'S SURPRISE

No one could guess Papa's surprise, not even Mimi. He refused to tell. "I'll just have to show ya!" he said, leading them to his SUV.

Nestled in the SUV's comfy leather seats, they rode past lovely lagoons that were chartreuse green with duckweed. Then Papa drove down a long lane of ancient oak trees that seemed to wag their gray beards at them as they passed. Finally, Papa pulled the SUV to a stop at the village dock.

Avery was beginning to wonder if Papa had discovered some amazing sea creature that had gotten confused and swam into the Palmetto Bluff boathouse. He slowly swung open the doors that groaned on huge hinges.

"Meet the new woman in my life!" Papa exclaimed with a flourish as his cowboy hat directed their eyes toward a brand-new, sparkling white Sea Ray boat. Painted across the back in lipstick red was *The Mimi*.

Mimi couldn't have been more surprised if she were looking at a genuine mermaid right in front of her. "She's beautiful!" she exclaimed.

"Just like the woman's she's named for," Papa said proudly. "Who wants to go for a cruise?"

"You're not gonna try to catch any hammerhead sharks, are you?" Avery asked.

"Not as long as they don't try to catch me," Papa said with a laugh.

The Mimi rocked like a cradle as they all climbed in. Papa took the wheel, and soon the boat was backing out of the boathouse and sputtering down the river. She was not nearly as large and powerful as *The Worm*, but riding on her was much more relaxing.

Evan and Noah each took a turn at the wheel. Papa poured his homemade lemonade from the gallon jug in the cooler and Avery served it in paper cups.

"I wish I had my camera!" Mimi said as she spotted a red-bellied woodpecker climbing a tall pine.

Avery counted 11 turtles sunning on a log and laughed. "They look like tourists relaxing by the pool!"

Suddenly, Evan ran to the front of the boat, waving his arms wildly. Avery was never surprised at anything he did, but honestly, she couldn't tell what had set him off this time.

"Get out of here!" he yelled. "Fly away!"

The commotion caused a huge heron to flap its powerful wings and take to the air. Only after it was gone did Avery understand. She saw an alligator—and it must have been as long as Papa was tall. It slid down the muddy bank and slipped into the water with barely a sound.

"You saved that heron's life, Evan!" Avery said.

"Yeah!" Evan said proudly, strutting back to the wheel with Papa.

Avery shuddered at the thought of what the alligator's powerful jaws and teeth would have done to the bird.

When they reached a wide area of the river, Papa said it was time to turn back. "I think this is far enough for our maiden voyage," he said. "I'm still learning to use all the equipment. Next time, we'll take her all the way to Beaufort, or beyond!"

As the boat turned in the current, it bumped into an orange ball floating on the surface. Noah noticed it first. "That looks too small to be a buoy," he said.

"Why don't we pull it out and see," Avery suggested.

Mimi was taking her turn steering the boat and Evan had joined them at the rail. "Want me to dive in and get it?" Evan asked.

Remembering the alligator, Avery quickly said, "NO!" She picked up a pole lying on the deck and pulled the ball close enough to reach over the side and pick it up.

"It hasn't been here long," Noah said, noticing that the ball was clean with no algae growing on its sides. A string attached to the bottom of the ball dangled in the water. Avery pulled it up. "There's a note attached!" she said.

She quickly grabbed the plastic bag holding the note and dropped the ball back into the water. The note had three red stripes with a black "X" over the top. On top of that were the numbers 5 and 6 underlined. Beneath the stripes were numbers and letters: 31° 59.7'N/80° 35.7'W.

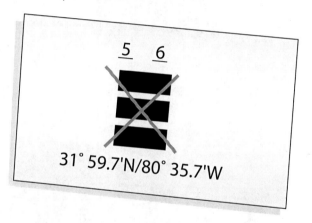

"This has to be some sort of clue!" Avery said. "But what does it mean and who was it meant for?"

Hilton Head's Harbour Town
Lighthouse is a beautiful sight!

10

GUPPIES AND GRITS

After their river cruise, Mimi prepared a supper of shrimp and grits. Avery asked if she could eat a sandwich instead.

"Grits are for breakfast," she had said. "And you put butter in them, not shrimp!"

Papa tried to convince her. "It's a Lowcountry specialty," he said. "One bite and you'll be hooked like a catfish on a cricket."

Evan didn't have to be begged. "I'll eat shrimp, even if they are swimming in grits," he said.

Noah teased Evan. "I bet you'd even eat guppies and grits."

Evan, who had just taken a swallow of iced tea, laughed so hard it came out of his nose and ran down his red and white striped t-shirt.

"Wow!" Avery said, amazed at Evan's trick. "I'll try the shrimp and grits, but I'm not sure I'll ever be able to drink tea again after seeing that!"

As soon as they had finished eating, the kids headed to the back porch to enjoy the sunset. Mimi served them chocolate chip cookies fresh from the oven. "Mmmmmm," Avery said. "The chips are still gooey, just the way I like them. You won't have to beg me to eat these!"

Avery looked at Evan, who was stuffing an entire cookie in his mouth at once. She could tell by his red nose that he'd spent too much time on the water recently. "Careful, Evan," she warned. "You're gonna have a burnt mouth to go with your burnt nose! With that red and white shirt and that glowing red nose, you look like the Harbour Town Light–" Avery stopped and pulled the note from the river out of her pocket.

"Did you mean lighthouse?" Evan asked.

"Yes!" Avery said. "These red and white marks on the clue must mean the lighthouse! Evan, why don't you go and get your iPad?"

Noah took the note from Avery. "But there's an 'X' over it," he said. "That could mean it's the spot where something is. Or, it could mean they crossed off the lighthouse because it's not the right spot."

Evan, who remembered the letters and numbers on the clue, began reading something on his iPad when he got back to the porch. "I think it has something to do with a lazy attitude," he said.

"Let me see," Avery said. Evan had Googled the correct combination of letters and numbers, but he couldn't read the big words correctly.

"Of course!" she said. "I should have recognized it. We studied this in school last year. The letters and numbers written under the lighthouse are **latitude** and **longitude**. This note gives the latitude and longitude for a spot somewhere near Hilton Head Island. The numbers 5 and 6 above the lighthouse don't make sense, though."

"So," Noah said. "Maybe whoever found that note was supposed to go to one of the lighthouses on Hilton Head Island? Since the red and white Harbour Town Lighthouse is crossed off, I think it means they were supposed to go to the old lighthouse that I told you about."

"But what about the ghost?" Evan asked, his knees wobbling.

Before Avery could scold Evan for being scared by a ghost story, she felt feathery fingers tickling her neck.

11

BOTHERSOME BUG

Avery flapped her arms like a crane about to take flight and pounded her feet on the wooden porch like a Broadway tap dancer.

Noah and Evan were entertained by the **animated** display.

"Don't just sit there," she cried. "Help me!"

The **commotion** drew Papa to the porch. "What in tarnation is going on out here?" he asked.

Evan and Noah shrugged. "I don't know what's wrong with her," Evan said. "I think she's having some sort of fit!"

Avery was now slapping at her neck and turning in circles. Papa grabbed her by the shoulders. "What is it, Avery?"

Avery's final slap sent something sailing out of her hair. It opened its wings in mid-air and flew to the porch column.

Papa laughed. "Is that all?" he said. "Why, it's just a big ol' palmetto bug."

Evan and Noah examined the glossy black bug. "Looks like a roach to me," Evan said. He held his finger beside it. "But I've never seen one this big. It's longer than my finger!"

"I see them all the time," Noah said. "They love to hang out on palmetto trees. They are nasty looking, but nothing to be afraid of."

"I'm afraid they're just part of life in these parts," Papa said. "You might call them another Lowcountry specialty."

"You're not planning to cook them with grits, are you, Papa?" Evan asked.

"Even if I wanted to, Mimi would never let me in the house with them," Papa said with a laugh. "But believe me, I'd never want to."

"My mom says that roaches have been around since the days of the dinosaurs," Noah said. "She's even found fossils of them."

"Well, I wish that whatever took out the dinosaurs had gotten the roach family, too!" Avery said as she combed her fingers through her disheveled hair. "Ooh, Oooh, Ooooh!" she said, turning in circles again. "What is that disgusting smell?"

"He must have sprayed ya!" Papa said.

"What!?" Avery asked.

"That's how they defend themselves," Noah said. "You attacked him and he sprayed you with his stink spray. Their nickname is skunk bug, you know."

"I didn't attack him!" Avery yelled as she ran through the door. Her voice continued to echo out to the porch. "Mimi! Where's the strawberry-scented shampoo!?"

The boys exploded with the laughter they'd been holding in. "I wish I had some of that stink spray," Evan said with a giggle. Papa scolded them for laughing at Avery, but turned his head so they wouldn't see him smiling.

When Avery returned smelling more like a strawberry than a stink bug, she was amazed that the boys were still looking at the palmetto bug. They were poking it with pine needles they'd plucked from the flowerbed.

"Does one of you want to get sprayed too?" she asked.

"He sprayed it all on you," Evan said with a grin. "His stink tank is empty now!"

"I've had enough of that bug," Avery said. She grabbed a magazine off Mimi's rocking chair and brushed the bug off the column and into the bushes. "Good riddance!" she shouted.

"But we wanted to see him fly again!" Evan whined.

"Fine," she said, leaning against the white porch column. "Leave your window open tonight and maybe he'll fly in and sleep with you!"

Avery suddenly pulled her hand away from the column. "Remind me to never lean on these things again," she said. "They're rough, Papa."

"They're made of tabby," Papa said. "It's a building material that's been used for centuries in this area.

"I didn't know it would get that hard," Evan said. "But I guess if you leave it in the sun long enough, it does."

"What else do you know about it?" Avery asked.

"I love the stuff!" Evan said. "Especially the salt water kind."

Now Avery understood. Evan was confused again.

"He didn't say taffy, Evan," Avery said. "He said tabby."

"Tabby, taffy," Evan said. "What's the difference?"

"Well, I think you seem to know what taffy is," Papa said. "Tabby is a kind of concrete that's made from lime, sand, and oyster shells."

Avery looked closely at the column. "I see the bits of oyster shells," she said. "They almost look like fossils.

Then, something occurred to Avery. "I guess you'd get awfully dusty making tabby, wouldn't you, Papa?" she asked.

"I've never made any," Papa said. "But I've mixed concrete. Every time I've done it, I'm always covered in that ol' grayish-white dust."

Avery remembered the dusty boots of the men at the fossil lecture and the clump of white mud that had dried in the parking lot at Buffalo's. *Could tabby have something to do with the missing fossils*, she wondered?

12

ENGINEERING A DIG

The next morning, Avery was in teacher mode again, and ready to discuss their STEM challenge to find a fossil—at least until they found an opportunity to go to Hilton Head to search for more clues.

"OK, we've talked about the science of finding fossils and we can use technology to help us with that," Avery said, green marker at the ready. "So I think we've covered the S and T of STEM. Now we need the E for engineering. First, we need an idea. That's the most important part."

"We could build a rocket so that when we find a fossil, we could tie it onto the rocket to yank it out of the ground," Noah said.

"I know you love rockets, Noah," Avery said, "but that sounds a little **impractical**. What if the rocket flew into the middle of the river and crashed? Or, what if it flew out of sight and we couldn't find it? We'd lose our fossil that we'd just found."

"I guess you're right," Noah said. "But I still want to build a rocket."

"What about you, Evan?" Avery asked. "Any ideas?

"We're gonna need a digger," Evan said. "Unless we find a fossil just lying on the ground."

"That's right," Avery said. "And we can't use Papa's shovel because that would be cheating. Mimi said we have to engineer our own tools."

Avery's marker squeaked on the board as she wrote: *Engineer a digger.*

"Any other ideas?" she asked, and then thought of one on her own. "The fossils will be dirty. We'll need some way to clean them."

"Since we want to find shark's teeth, maybe we should engineer a toothbrush," Evan said.

"We're not taking them to the dentist, Evan," Avery said.

"My mom uses a screen when she's looking for fossils," Noah said.

"Yeah, I've seen those things," Avery said. "They put the dirt in them and shake them. The dirt falls through and leaves the fossils. That would be a great tool!"

Avery wrote on the board: *Make a screen.*

"I've got another idea!" Avery said. "Since we'll be near the river, maybe we could use the current. Mimi and Papa won't let us get close enough to stick the screen directly into the river, but maybe we could make something that could bring the water to the screen."

"I like that idea!" Noah said.

Avery wrote: *Make water pipe.*

The kids set to work finding materials for their engineering projects. It wasn't long before the doorbell rang. It was Noah's mom, Mrs. Garcia. She looked tired—like she wasn't sleeping very well.

"Any luck with the fossils?" Mimi asked.

Mrs. Garcia sighed. "Nothing," she said. "After being hidden for millions of years, it's almost like they went back into hiding. Unfortunately, I don't have any idea where to look this time."

Avery thought about the hamburger wrapper note. It had said something about millions of years, too. She still felt that Sam, the assistant, knew something about all this. But Mrs. Garcia seemed to trust him.

"I have the day off," Mrs. Garcia said. "Mr. Garcia had to go to the NOAA station for a while, but I'm meeting him there. We want to give the kids a day of fun on Hilton Head. Maybe it'll take our minds off our troubles," she added.

Avery and Noah exchanged a high-five. "That's exactly where we need to go to check out that clue!" Avery whispered with excitement.

"That sounds like a wonderful idea!" Mimi said. "I'm a little jealous."

"Why don't you and Papa come along, too?" Mrs. Garcia said.

"We'd really love to," Mimi said. "But unfortunately, I have a deadline to meet for my new book. Maybe next time."

"Am I coming back here, after we go to Hilton Head?" Noah asked his mom. "You know, we're still working on our STEM project."

"We'd love for him to continue staying here with Avery and Evan," Mimi said.

Noah gave his mom a look that said, "PLEEEEEASE!"

"OK," Mrs. Garcia said. "As long as you're working on a project."

"You don't mind if I borrow your binoculars, do you, Mimi?" Avery asked. She was already trotting to get them off the hook where they hung by the back door.

"You can use them as long as you tell me about any unusual birds you spot," Mimi said.

"Deal," Avery replied. She hung the binoculars around her neck and pulled her hair out from under the strap.

As soon as the kids were out the door, Mimi went to the kitchen. That's when she noticed that something had been rummaging through the garbage. Can labels littered the floor. "Clue!" she yelled at the family dog. "You're in big trouble!"

Mimi went to the broom closet to sweep up the mess, but the broom was missing!

"Papa!" she yelled. "Papa? Did you take my broom?"

"Come here!" Papa yelled. He was crawling like a turtle behind the bushes planted by the back porch.

"I don't think my broom would be back there," Mimi remarked.

"I'm looking for the screen off one of the windows," Papa said. "It's missing!"

13

MAGNETIC HIGHWAYS

The kids convinced Mrs. Garcia to let them go to the top of Harbour Town Lighthouse before they picked up Mr. Garcia at the NOAA station.

"I can see for miles!" proclaimed Avery. From the top of the lighthouse, she surveyed the landscape with Mimi's binoculars, searching for landmarks she might recognize.

Evan, who had bought a pirate's spyglass in the lighthouse gift shop, pretended the observation deck was the crow's nest of a pirate ship. He aimed the spyglass at a section of white, sandy beach. "Ahoy there, maties!" he cried. "What are those ropes in the distance?"

Noah grabbed the viewing piece and took a look. "They are set up to keep people away," he said. "It might be a loggerhead sea turtle nesting site."

"The loggerhead is South Carolina's state reptile," Mrs. Garcia said. "It's on the **endangered** species list. That's why it's so important to protect areas where turtles might build nests. During the summer months, people along the beach are even asked to keep their outdoor lights turned off. The bright lights can confuse the turtles. The little hatchlings can be attracted to the artificial lights and crawl away from the ocean instead of toward it."

With his question answered, Evan took off running around the deck. When he stopped beside Avery, he was panting harder than Clue after he'd chased a rabbit. "I...counted...eight," he said.

"Eight what?" Avery asked.

"This lighthouse...has...eight sides," Evan said between breaths. "Hey! That makes it the shape of an octagon!"

"That's a type of polygon," Noah said.

"Polly want a cracker?" Evan squawked, flapping his arms, much to the aggravation of nearby tourists.

"You'll probably learn about that in school next year," Noah said. He was more interested in looking for clues than explaining shape families to Evan.

"See anything else interesting?" Noah asked Avery.

"Yeah," she said. "There's a funny-looking bird I can tell Mimi about. It's black and white—almost like a penguin. But it has a long orange beak that looks like a straw for drinking milkshakes. And...it has white, skinny legs like Evan's!"

"Must be built for speed," Evan said, looking down to admire his legs.

"That's an American Oystercatcher," Mrs. Garcia explained. "You're lucky to see one. Like so many other birds that nest on the shore, their numbers are decreasing. They've lost a lot of their **habitat** to human development."

"I guess they like to eat oysters," Avery said.

"Yes," Mrs. Garcia said. "They like all kinds of mollusks."

Evan thought about the slimy, slippery oysters he'd seen Papa eating raw and snickered mischievously. "I'd call them American booger eaters," he said.

Avery was growing too frustrated to laugh at Evan's joke. They hadn't found any clues. "I guess you were right," she told Noah. "Maybe the X on the note was crossing off this lighthouse. It was a sneaky way of telling someone to go to the other lighthouse. That's where we need to go!"

When they got to the station to pick up Mr. Garcia, he was in the back with the pups. "Just trying to get a few of them tagged," he said, poking a flat metal tag through one of their fins.

"That tag looks different than the one you put on the shark in the ocean," Avery said.

"It is," Mr. Garcia explained as he dried his hands. "These tags are only for identification, not for tracking. Hopefully, if these guys can be caught later, we can record data on their growth."

Evan was staring into the tank, watching the pups swim in a circle. "Don't they ever get tired?" he asked.

"If they stopped swimming, they would drown," Mr. Garcia explained. "Swimming keeps the water going through their gills. That's how they get oxygen."

"Well at least they don't ever have to take baths!" Evan said. "That would be great!"

"No, but they do get cleaned," Mr. Garcia said. "There are several species of fish that live in reefs known as cleaner fish."

"Like angel fish!" Noah said.

"That's right," Mr. Garcia said. "The sharks swim up to the cleaner fish and lean on their side to show their bellies. We think this is how they let the cleaner fish know they won't eat them! The cleaner fish then get busy eating the parasites off the sharks as well as cleaning any wounds they might have."

"Maybe I should get some cleaner fish to live in my bathtub!" Evan said.

Avery giggled at the thought. "You get so dirty the fish would probably need to go on a diet after cleaning you," she said.

Avery continued watching the little sharks swim. "I just can't get over their weird heads," she said.

"Not all scientists agree about why they're shaped that way," Mr. Garcia said. "Some think it helps them navigate through the water and turn quickly. Others believe that having their eyes so far apart helps them see prey better. Another theory is that the cephalofoil—that's the head—uses its special sensors to pick up electrical and magnetic impulses, or signals. Since other animals give off electrical impulses, it might help the hammerhead find food."

"Tell them about the magnetic highways," Mrs. Garcia suggested.

"Well, when lava seeps out of the earth's crust, it hardens into lines of basalt on the ocean floor," Mr. Garcia said. "These strips of basalt are magnetic. Some researchers think the hammerheads may follow these magnetic lines when they migrate."

"Just like we drive on highways to get where we're going!" Noah said.

"That's right," Mrs. Garcia said.

"Maybe one of you will grow up to be a scientist and answer a lot of the questions we have now," said Mr. Garcia.

"That's too much information for my head to hold," Evan said. "Let's go and see the other lighthouse."

"What lighthouse?" Mr. Garcia asked.

"The one with the ghost!" Evan said.

"You must be talking about the Rear Range Lighthouse," Mr. Garcia said. "That's on a golf course." He looked at his wife and smiled. "A round of golf would be nice."

"It's at Palmetto Dunes Resort," Mrs. Garcia said. "Sam works there on weekends at the gatehouse. He'd let us in to see the old lighthouse."

"Sam?" Avery asked, surprised to hear that her number one suspect worked at the same place they hoped to find a clue.

"You remember my assistant," Mrs. Garcia said. "He has to work on weekends to earn money for college."

Avery whispered to Noah. "I sure hope we find something there other than ghosts and golf balls!"

Baby loggerhead turtle heading
to the ocean!

14

GHOSTS AND GOLF BALLS

Mrs. Garcia was relieved that Sam was working at the gatehouse. "We've got some kids here who want to see the old lighthouse," she said. "Think you could let us in to take a look?"

"And maybe hit a few golf balls?" Mr. Garcia quickly added. "I just happen to have my clubs."

Sam hesitated and looked at the kids. "Why do you want to go to the lighthouse?" he asked.

Avery wasn't about to say what she was thinking...*to look for clues that prove you're the fossil thief!* Instead, she smiled sweetly. "We want to see if there's really a ghost there!"

"I'll call someone," he said. "You need permission to go in the lighthouse."

After Sam had made the call, he waved them through the gate.

"Thanks, Sam," Mrs. Garcia said. "I owe you a favor."

"I told them you were important scientists," Sam said, "who needed a break."

On the way to the golf course, Mrs. Garcia admitted concerns about her assistant. "I'm worried about Sam," she said. "He hasn't been himself lately."

"He's always been sort of an unconventional kid," Mr. Garcia said.

"He's quiet," Mrs. Garcia said. "But he's becoming a great paleontologist."

Avery kept her opinions to herself.

After parking the car, the kids followed Mr. and Mrs. Garcia to the clubhouse. "I've never played this course," Mr. Garcia said. "Looks pretty tough."

"Not to me," Mrs. Garcia teased. "Do you want to see who can do the best on the first few holes?"

"The lighthouse is down there," Noah said. Avery could barely see it peeking above the tree tops.

"Mind if we go and check out the lighthouse...while you beat Mr. Garcia?" Avery said with a smile.

"OK," Mrs. Garcia said. "But be careful. We'll be there soon!"

As the kids walked toward the lighthouse, Avery asked Noah, "So, aren't you gonna tell us the ghost story?"

"Oh yeah," Noah replied. "Back in the 1800s, the light in the lighthouse came from an oil lantern. The legend goes that during a hurricane, the light keeper climbed to the top of the lighthouse to add oil to the lantern. Just as he got to the lantern room, a gust of wind hit. It shattered the window and scared him so bad he had a heart attack.

"Now, here's the good part," Noah continued. "The man had a daughter. When her father didn't return, she went to check on him. He was dying, but he asked her to keep the light burning during the storm. She kept the light burning, but she was so sad and exhausted that she died a short time later. Since then, people claim that they've seen a girl in a blue dress in the lighthouse, especially on dark and stormy nights."

"Cool!" Evan said.

"I'm glad it's daylight and sunny," Avery said. But when they walked into a grove of tall pines, she didn't feel quite as confident. The lighthouse was certainly something out of a ghost story. Tall and gray, its iron frame looked like a giant skeleton. Towering above them, Avery thought it might lean over and say, "Booooo!"

"Where do you think we should look for a clue?" Avery asked. No one answered. *Noah and Evan were gone.*

Looking up, up, up at the Hilton Head Rear Range Lighthouse!

15

112 STEPS

"OOOOOOOOOOh! I'm the ghost of the lighthouse..." a quivering voice oozed from the bushes.

Avery jumped. She was deciding whether to run straight, left, or right, when she heard a giggle—the kind that comes from a pesky brother. "EVAN!" she yelled.

"I told him not to scare you right after you'd heard a ghost story," Noah said.

Avery took a deep breath and said, "Whew! Now I know how that light keeper felt when the glass shattered and scared him to death! But Evan," she added, "if you're going to play the ghost of the lighthouse, you're supposed to wear a blue dress!"

"Never!" Evan said.

"Anyway," Avery said, "why'd you two disappear?"

"I wanted to check something," Noah said. "I got to thinking about the 5 and the 6 that were written on the note we found. My hunch was right! This lighthouse is right between the 5th and 6th holes of the golf course!"

"That tells us we're right where we should be!" Avery said. "Let's look for clues."

The kids approached the skeletal lighthouse cautiously. It had been standing in the same spot for more than a hundred years, but to Avery, it still looked like it might start walking.

"One, two, three, four, five, six. This lighthouse has six sides," Evan said. "It's a hexagon—that's another 6, you know. But how did the light keeper get to the tower? I don't see a ladder anywhere!"

"I think there are stairs in that big tube in the center of its legs," Noah said.

"Do they still guide ships with this lighthouse?" Avery asked.

"No," Noah said. "They haven't used it for a very long time."

As the kids walked around the tower, they suddenly, heard something echoing inside the tube. "I think someone is using those stairs right now!" Avery whispered.

The legs of the lighthouse rested on round concrete pillars. They were just the right size for the kids to hide behind. They listened. The heavy footsteps were getting closer and closer to the bottom. Avery held her breath as a doorknob squeaked. She motioned for Evan to be still. A man walked down the short set of steps from the stairwell door to the ground. On his head was a yellow hardhat. His shoes were heavy work boots—the kind Avery had seen men wear at construction sites. Jeans and a dark green shirt completed the outfit. A coating of white dust looked like dandruff on his dark shirt.

The kids watched the man walk to a small building near the tower. It was built of reddish-brown brick with a green metal roof.

"Who do you think he is?" Noah whispered.

"I couldn't see his face," Avery answered. "But he's dressed like those men were at the fossil lecture. The men I saw talking to Sam."

"You don't like Sam, do you?" Noah asked.

"I really don't know him," Avery said. "But I think he knows something about those missing fossils. There are just too many **coincidences**."

"Maybe we should go and get Mom and Dad," Noah said.

"Not yet," Avery said. "This is their day to relax. They've had too much to worry about lately."

"True." Noah said. "I've really been concerned about them."

"I think we should climb the tower stairs and see what he was doing up there," Avery suggested.

"I don't think Miss Blue Dress would like that!" Evan said, backing away.

"Yeah, and what if that guy comes back?" Noah said. "Then we'd be trapped."

"We're small and fast," Avery said, "like little mice. I think we could slip around him and get back down the stairs before he could catch us."

"But what if he has a mousetrap?" Evan asked.

"I have my phone, Evan," Avery said. "We can call for help."

The kids slipped out of their hiding spot and ran to the tower door. Avery twisted the knob, fully expecting it to be locked. She gasped in surprise. It wasn't!

The three crept up the stairs. Thankfully, their flip-flops didn't make nearly as much noise on the stairs as the man's boots had made.

Evan counted the steps as they climbed. They stopped on step 56 to catch their breath. "I hope there's something up there," Evan said. "This is a workout!"

They had just reached step 94, when they heard the door open below them. "He's coming!" Noah warned.

They scurried up 18 more steps to find themselves in the lantern room. "There's no place to hide in here!" Evan said.

"Quick!" Avery said. "Help me open this window!"

The window was stuck, almost as if the Blue Dress Ghost was holding it down on the other side, not wanting to let them out. "We've got to do this!" Avery said. "On three, use your muscles! One, two, three!"

The tired old window creaked open just wide enough for them to squeeze through. They mashed themselves like squashed sardines beside the window so the man couldn't see them if he looked out. The deck beneath their feet was made of wooden boards with cracks between each board. "Whoa!" Evan said. "It's a long way down!"

"Shhh!" Avery cautioned.

They heard the man reach the lantern room. They could tell by the *beeps* that he was dialing someone on his phone.

"Yeah, this is Roger," the children heard him say. "I got another batch started. It should be ready to go out tomorrow night if all's clear—just give the signal."

Roger stalked around the room, stopping every few steps. Outside, the kids held their positions...and their breath.

"Huh! That's weird," he said into the phone. "Maybe there is something to that silly old ghost story. I'm sure the window was closed last time I was up here and now it's open. Hang on! Umpfh! Good. Got it shut nice and tight."

As his footsteps ebbed away toward the door, the kids heard Roger say, "Hey, the sharks doing their job? Great! Yep, they're adding another piece right now. Another great hiding place! Good deal. Quarry, then home. Bye!"

The kids heard Roger stomp slowly back down the stairs.

16

EXPLODING JELLYFISH?

The kids watched Roger leave the grove of pine trees and stroll across the golf course before they were brave enough to struggle to open the window and climb back inside.

"Better make sure we close it back this time," Noah said. "Or would it be better to leave it open and really scare this guy, Roger?"

"Did you hear what he was saying?!" Avery asked.

"Yeah," Evan said. "He said something about a batch. That makes me think of a batch of Mimi's brownies! Do you think he's making brownies? He said they're going out tomorrow night. Maybe we should come back and get some. I love brownies—especially Mimi's praline brownies."

"I really don't think he's making brownies, Evan," said Avery.

Noah was thinking. "The strangest thing he said was something about the sharks."

"Yes!" Avery said. "How could sharks do a job?"

"I thought of a job for them," Evan said. "Remember when we first saw the pups and I said they'd make good watchdogs?"

"Hmmmm," Avery said. "You just might be on to something, Evan."

"Could you make out the last of what he said?" Noah asked. "I thought I heard him say something about a quarry, but I'm not sure."

"That was it," Avery said. "I was standing closest to the window and I heard it clearly. It sounded like he was going to a quarry after he left here and then going home."

"Were we talking about quarries recently?" Evan asked. "Something about that word rings a bell."

Avery refreshed his memory. "It was when we were trying to decide where to look for fossils, remember? We learned that a good place to look for fossils is in a limestone quarry."

"Oh, yeah!" Evan said, making his tenth trip around the lantern room. "Wow!" he said, stopping. " There's an amazing view of the ocean from here!"

"It would be kind of dumb if you couldn't see the ocean from a lighthouse," Avery said. "That would mean the ships couldn't see the lighthouse from the ocean!"

"Oh, yeah!" Evan said again. "Guess I wasn't thinking, or at least I was thinking about something else. Getting back to the limestone thing, didn't Papa say something about limestone that night on the porch when the bug attacked you?"

"Yes," Avery said. " I think he told us that tabby is made from lime, sand, and oyster shells..."

Before Avery could say anything else, a loud BOOM echoed across the water and made the old lighthouse shudder under their feet.

"What was that?!" Avery asked, looking at Noah for an answer.

"It definitely came from the ocean," he answered, and laughed. "Maybe it was a cannonball jellyfish exploding!"

"What?" Avery asked. "I don't understand."

"I was trying to be funny like Evan," he said, turning red. "Cannonball jellyfish are shaped like cannonballs, but they don't really explode. It's a bad joke."

"Then, what was the noise?" Avery asked. "I wish I hadn't left the binoculars in the car."

"I've got something better," said Evan. He whipped his pirate spyglass out of his belt and stared through it out to sea. "There's a big ship thing out there. Looks like a crane."

"Let me see," Noah said, taking the spyglass. "Oh, I know what that is. That barge is about to drop a big metal shipping container into the ocean. It must have hit the side of the barge to cause that noise."

"Shouldn't we tell the authorities?" Avery asked. "Isn't polluting the ocean against the law?"

"This is the only good kind of pollution," Noah said. "They're building an artificial reef. They use old ships, tanks, subway cars—all kinds of things. It makes a good home for the fish."

"Including sharks?" Evan asked.

"Yes!" Noah said. "My dad says it's a good thing."

KERSPLASH! "There it goes!" Evan said. "It's sinking fast!"

"That's because they cut lots of holes into them so the fish can swim in and out easily," Noah said.

As the boys watched the container disappear beneath the waves, Avery looked around the lantern room. When she reached the window where they had crawled out, she noticed a piece of paper lying on the floor. "Look at this," she said. "Roger must have dropped it when he closed the window!"

"What does it say?" Noah asked.

Avery read the note:

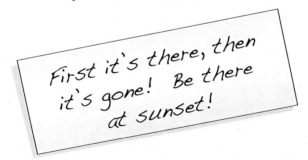

First it's there, then it's gone! Be there at sunset!

17

GHOSTLY GRAVE?

"I guess it would have to be something that appears and disappears," Avery said as they trudged down the lighthouse stairs.

"Maybe a magician's rabbit?" Evan suggested.

Avery rolled her eyes. "What does that have to do with fossils or sharks?"

"They do have those sharp teeth!" Evan said. He stuck his front teeth over his bottom lip and gave a Bugs Bunny pose.

"Hmmm, what's another word for disappearing?" Noah asked.

"Vanishing?" Avery suggested.

"Yes!" Noah answered. "There's a place called Vanishing Island, but it's not around here. It's really just a large sandbar that appears and disappears with the ebb and flow of the tide."

"What if there's a sandbar like that near here?" Avery asked. "Maybe there's one near the reef! That sounds like something we need to research."

Noah pushed on the door leading out of the stairway tube. "Whew!" he said. "I was really afraid it might be locked."

"Is that where the lighthouse keeper and his daughter are buried?" Evan asked. He pointed to a strange brick structure only a few feet high with a curved round top.

"That gives me the creeps!" Avery said. "Maybe it's where the Blue Dress Ghost sleeps during the day!"

"Here's a sign that tells about it," Noah said. "It's not a grave. It's a cistern. It's where they used to keep water."

"So it's where the Blue Dress Ghost comes to get a drink of water!" Avery said.

"I wonder if there's anything in there now," Evan said. He shouted *"HELLLOOO IN THERE!"* through one of the holes on the end of the cistern. His voice echoed all around the structure before it finally faded away. He shrugged his shoulders. "Sounds empty to me."

"Let's see if we can get into that little brick building!" Avery said, leading the way. "Roger went inside there." When she turned the doorknob, she was disappointed. Not only was the door locked, there was an extra padlock near the top.

"Maybe we can at least peek in the windows," Evan suggested.

The kids snuck behind the bushes that grew under the window and peered inside. "It's dark in there," Avery said. "Maybe the flashlight app on my phone will help."

She shined the light through the dirty glass. "Interesting!" she said. There was a long table in the one-room building. It was covered in the same white dust that Avery had seen on Roger's shirt.

"What are those cup-looking things?" Evan asked. "They kind of remind me of Mimi's Jell-O molds."

"I was thinking the same thing," Avery said.

"HEY, KIDS!" they heard someone yell.

"That's my mom," Noah said. "We'd better go and meet them."

"Have you kids had a good time?" Mrs. Garcia asked. "That old lighthouse sure looks creepy. I don't think I'd want to go inside."

"Especially not if someone's chasing you," Avery muttered so Mrs. Garcia wouldn't hear.

As they left, Avery suspected she had not seen the last of the Rear Range Lighthouse.

18

MOLDY THEORIES

The next morning at Mimi and Papa's, the kids knew they should be working on their STEM project, but Avery had more important tasks to do.

She was checking the tide tables on Evan's iPad. "It fits!" she said. "Low tide is late this afternoon. Should be right around sunset. If there is a sandbar out there, that would be about when it should appear."

"But we don't have a way to check it out," Noah said. "My parents had work to do today. There's no way they'd take us back to the lighthouse, and even if they did, that's too far away from the water to investigate a sand bar."

"Do you think your dad might take us out on *The Worm*?" Evan asked. "I promise not to eat grilled cheese!"

"No," Noah said. "The crew's off today."

"There is one other option," Avery said. She and Evan looked at each other and in unison cried: *"The Mimi!"*

"Good idea!" Noah said. "But maybe we should wait until after lunch to make the suggestion, so we can be where we want to be at sunset."

After she'd made Papa triple-quadruple check and pinkie promise that no palmetto bugs were lurking about, Avery and the boys headed to the screened porch. Avery wanted to get another good look at those tabby columns. "If something like tabby could be shaped into columns," she said, "then it could be shaped into anything."

"Yeah," Noah said, smacking a big wad of purple bubble gum. "It's like cement, so it could be made into any shape. Haven't you seen those cement picnic tables and benches and things? I've even seen cement dogs and dolphins!"

Evan was Googling something on his iPad. "First you have to make a mold," he said. "Watch this video I found."

After they'd watched the video, the theory that had formed in Avery's mind was becoming clearer.

Noah created a mini demonstration. "If I took my bubblegum and pressed it over my chin, like this," he said, spreading the wad under his bottom lip, "I could make a mold."

When he pulled the bubblegum off, Avery and Evan could see that there was a ridge in the gum made by the dimple in his chin. "If I turn this over and let it harden," Noah added, "I could pour something like plaster of Paris in it. When the plaster dried, I'd have a copy of my chin."

"Just like Mimi's Jell-O molds," Avery said. "Just like we saw in the little brick building!"

"Couldn't someone do the same thing with valuable fossils that you're doing with your chin?" Avery asked. "I think that whoever stole those fossils is making copies of them!"

"I think you're right!" Noah said. "Maybe they're using ground-up limestone from a quarry and mixing it with something to make fakes!"

"And the sharks could be the watchdogs that are guarding them!" Evan suggested.

"But how could you possibly train sharks to do something like that?" Avery asked. *There were still so many unanswered questions!*

19

LUNCH AND MUNCH

"Come and eat lunch!" Mimi called to the kids on the porch. "I've got grilled cheese and tomato soup!"

"Oh, no!" Evan moaned. "If we can convince Papa to take us out in the boat, I'll starve. You know what will happen if I eat grilled cheese!"

"Yes!" Avery said. "Just eat lots of soup. We need those cans for our STEM project, anyway."

It didn't take much persuading to convince Papa to take them for another cruise. He'd been practicing his navigating skills and now felt confident to go out into what he called "Big Water."

"I love spending time with my two favorite ladies," Papa said, "Mimi and *The Mimi!*" He pulled off his big cowboy hat and plopped a sea captain's hat on his head.

Avery was surprised. "Life in the Lowcountry is changing you from a cowboy to a captain, Papa!" she said.

By late afternoon, they were happily coasting through Calibogue Sound. The lowering sun glimmered gold on the water like fireflies trapped in honey.

The kids had told Papa they wanted to sail over the reef where they'd seen the container sunk. "Maybe we can get a glimpse of a hammerhead," Evan had said.

Papa steered in that direction. "That's odd," he said after a while. "I wonder what all these small buoys are for?"

"Evan, what are you doing?" asked Avery. She stared at the string of peppers he was stringing along behind the boat as if he were trolling for fish.

Evan shrugged. "I read that Native Americans in Panama hung peppers behind their canoes to protect themselves from sharks," he explained. "Good thing I found these growing in Papa's garden, huh?"

Avery noticed that the orange balls floating in the water looked just like the one they'd pulled out of the water the other day. "We need to grab one of those when we get a chance," Avery said. Once more, she grabbed the pole she'd used before. When *The Mimi* passed one, she waited until it was close to the boat's stern and hooked it. When she pulled the ball out of the water there was something dangling from a wire. But it wasn't a note this time.

Before the kids could pull it into the boat for a closer look, an enormous hammerhead shark rocketed out of the water! Its gnashing teeth wrapped around the pole, snapping off the end. As the shark tumbled back into the sea, it sent a shower of chilly, salty water raining down on the kids.

When Mimi looked back, all she saw were drenched kids with shocked expressions. "Don't look so surprised," she said. "If you hit the water with the pole, of course you're going to get wet!"

"What was that?" Avery asked, still in shock from what had just happened.

"It was a SHARK!" Evan yelled. "And I thought hammerheads were supposed to be laid back!"

"It acted like something had upset it," Avery said. "And I don't think it was the pole. Did you see that thing dangling from the ball?"

"Yeah!" Noah said. "It almost looked like some sort of microphone."

"Maybe someone's piping music underwater, and he didn't like that tune!" Evan said.

Suddenly, the *The Mimi* lurched. The kids grabbed the rail to keep from flipping over into the water, glad that Papa always insisted they wear life vests.

"What happened, Papa?" Avery asked. Papa was frantically turning the wheel.

"It feels like the hull hit something underwater!" he shouted. "I think we're stuck!"

Avery felt water swirling around her ankles. "We've got bigger problems than being stuck, Papa!" she said. "We're sinking!"

20

GREEN-EYED MONSTER

Papa immediately called the Coast Guard on his marine radio. Meanwhile, Mimi and the kids grabbed buckets and started bailing water.

The more Avery thought of the shark's sharp teeth, the faster she bailed. And the faster she bailed, the faster the water seemed to rise—until suddenly it stopped and started to **recede**.

"What is going on here?" Mimi asked.

Suddenly, as Avery stared over the stern of the boat, she understood. The last rays of sunlight gleamed on what looked like a mirage, but was really a stretch of sand and rock—right there in the middle of the water!

She tugged on Noah's shirt. "That's it, isn't it?!" she whispered. *"The thing that is there and then isn't."* Avery checked the time on her phone. "And it's right on schedule, right at low tide."

"I guess some of those orange balls I saw were buoys to keep me away from this," Papa said with his head in his hands. "I just thought they were marking crab pots. Well, the Coast Guard should be here soon."

"Mind if we go for a little walk on the sandbar?" Avery asked Mimi. "This might be a good spot to look for fossils!"

"Stay right in the middle," Mimi cautioned. "It might disappear again quickly."

As they walked, Avery shined her flashlight app on the water. Circling the sandbar were pointed fins—shark fins!

"There must be hundreds!" Evan said. "I'm suddenly not liking this sand bar. Where's the Coast Guard already?!"

"That is very strange to see so many sharks in one place," Noah remarked.

Their only choices to escape the sharks were the sandbar, or a boat that might sink faster than the sandbar. The kids walked a little farther, until Avery noticed a light blinking from the shore.

"That looks like it's coming from the old lighthouse!" she said. "I thought you said it didn't work anymore, Noah!"

"It may be coming from the old lighthouse, but it's not big enough to be a lighthouse light," Noah said.

The light blinked again. This time it was green, like the old lighthouse had changed from a skeleton to a green-eyed monster. In a moment, they could hear a speedboat zipping toward them.

"Let's get back to the boat!" Avery cried.

They started running, but Evan caught his foot on something and fell hard. When Avery reached down to help him up, she could see something round embedded in the sand. She turned on her flashlight again and saw that it was a heavy metal lid.

"C'mon!" she said, helping Evan back to his feet.

But before they could reach *The Mimi*, the tiny speedboat had pulled up on the opposite end of the sand strip. Two men in wetsuits jumped out.

"Hey!" one of them said. "What's that boat doing over there?"

"That voice sounds familiar!" Noah said. As the men drew closer, they could tell that it was Jack, the electronics expert at NOAA. This time he wasn't so cheerful. "What are you doing here?" he asked.

"I think that's what we should be asking you!" Avery said.

Before they could answer, *The Mimi* and the sandbar were bathed in a powerful, white spotlight. "THIS IS THE COAST GUARD," a loudspeaker blared.

The men in wetsuits ran for their speedboat. "You need to catch those men!" Avery cried to the Guardsman who had already climbed aboard *The Mimi*.

"What's going on?" Mimi asked.

"I'll explain everything," Avery told her grandmother.

21

FINS AND FOSSILS

Noah's parents, who had received a call from the Coast Guard, picked them up at the dock.

With *The Mimi* towed safely to shore for repairs, Papa could finally relax as he sipped iced cocoa on the back porch.

"The Coast Guard said they found a lot of electronic equipment buried in the sand bar," Mr. Garcia said. "I can't believe that Jack would get involved with a ring of criminals like that. He's such a brilliant man to waste his talents that way."

"Jack took everything he learned about shark behavior and tagging," Avery explained, "and reprogrammed the sharks' tags so that when they picked up signals from those buoys, the sharks would do nothing but swim around and around that artificial reef."

"That's right," Noah said. "He also reprogrammed the remote entry for the van. That's how his cronies stole the fossils to begin with."

"The sharks made perfect guard dogs for all the fake fossils they'd been hiding down there," Evan said.

"But why did those men want to hide the fake fossils in the water, Mom?" Noah asked.

"To make them look old," Mrs. Garcia said. "It sounds like they hid the fake fossils at several different reefs. They moved them from place to place so no one would catch up to them.

"I'm just thankful you kids suggested looking in that cistern for the originals," she added. "Who would have thought they were just using the real fossils to make fakes, instead of stealing them to sell?"

"I guess they could keep selling the copies for years," Mr. Garcia said, "and have a steady source of income."

"I'm just glad that Sam is picking them up right now," Mrs. Garcia said.

Avery looked concerned. "Are you sure Sam isn't involved?" she finally asked.

"He was being blackmailed!" Mrs. Garcia explained. "He first met some of the thieves when he visited the quarry to ask them to be on the lookout for fossils. When they learned about the high value of some of the fossils we have, they told him they would destroy the fossils one by one if he told anyone of their plans. Sam was willing to do anything to save those fossils!

"At first, they told Sam they only wanted to borrow the fossils for two weeks," Mrs. Garcia added. "Then they got greedy and kept them."

Avery remembered the note written on the hamburger wrapper. "So it was Sam who wrote that note about borrowed time!" she exclaimed.

Then, Avery felt guilty about the suspicions she'd had about Sam. "Can we invite Sam to our fossil expedition and picnic?" she asked.

22

PRICELESS

Mimi, Papa, and Mr. and Mrs. Garcia watched the kids set up their fossil-finding project. They had carefully kept all their "equipment" hidden so that it would be a surprise to the grownups. They had chosen an area of the May River where the water had changed course through the years and had left a muddy **shoal**.

"This is our digger," Evan said proudly as he showed them a big soup ladle duct-taped to a long yellow handle.

"Another mystery solved," Mimi said with a smile. "Now I know what happened to my broom. I'd recognize that yellow handle anywhere!"

Next, Noah and Avery pulled out a frame made from four boards. In the center was a screen. "That's why I haven't been able to raise a certain window lately," Papa said, recognizing the screen off his porch window.

The final piece of equipment was a curved tube, which the kids had assembled out of different sizes of cans. They had cut the tops and bottoms out of the cans and had taped them together with duct tape.

"I owe Clue an apology!" Mimi said. "He's been blamed for an awful lot of garbage can rummaging lately."

The kids placed the framed screen on some large rocks to hold it off the ground. Then, they crossed two sticks and taped them in the center to hold the tube at the right angle to catch river water. Soon, water was pouring on top of the screen.

"It works!" Avery cried.

"Just like rocket science!" Noah said.

Evan plopped a big scoop of Lowcountry pluff mud on top of the screen. Then Avery and Noah used their hands to rub the mud through the screen. "Nothing yet," Avery said. "Keep digging!"

After digging all morning, the most interesting things the kids found were a smooth pebble that Evan thought was shaped just like Papa's nose, and two pull-tabs off soda cans.

When they stopped for a picnic lunch, Sam joined them. With the missing fossils back where they belonged, he seemed to Avery like a different person. He was even smiling.

"Don't give up!" he encouraged the kids. "Sharks are like teeth-making machines. They have rows of teeth. They often lose a tooth when they're catching prey. But every time they lose one, another tooth moves forward to take its place. Would you believe that some sharks can grow as many as 30,000 teeth in their lifetime?"

"That's right," Mr. Garcia said. "I'd say your odds of finding a tooth are pretty good."

After lunch the kids got back to work. Evan had dug until he was standing in the middle of a hole.

"You're getting shorter and shorter!" Avery teased.

"I read the flat-shaped head of the hammerhead shark might let it use sonar to track its prey," Evan said. "I think Mom has sonar. She can detect when I'm doing something I'm not supposed to way too easily."

"You mean like the *ping ping ping* you hear in submarine movies?" asked Avery. But before Evan could answer, she gasped.

Evan plopped yet another big scoop of mud right on Avery's hand. "OUCH!" she screamed. "I think something bit me!"

23

TERRIFIC TOOTH

Noah swished his hand through the glob of mud. "Something did bite you!" he said excitedly. "A tooth!"

"We found one!!" Avery cried. She placed the tooth beneath the water trickling from their engineered tube. "And it's a beauty!"

The root, or part that would have held the tooth in the gum, was rough and a dirty beige color. The tooth itself was dark gray with tiny white streaks running down the center. It was as slick as glass except for the serrated edges.

"See, Mimi," Evan said "you could use it as a bread knife!"

"We've used science, technology and engineering," Avery said. "And now it's time for the M—math!"

She took the measuring tape she had borrowed from Papa's toolbox and held it beside the tooth. "It's 2-½ inches long!"

Avery remembered the formula Mrs. Garcia had told them. "Two-and-one-half inches multiplied by 10 is 25," she said, making quick calculations in her head. "This shark was about 25 feet long!"

Evan took the measuring tape and a stick and drew a line in the mud on the shore.

"What are you doing?" Avery asked.

"I want to see what 25 feet looks like," he said.

"Wow!" Evan said. "Let's see—I was about four feet tall when Mimi measured me a few weeks ago. How many of me would it take to equal 25 feet?"

"It would take six of you, plus one more foot," Avery said.

"Great job!" Mimi and Papa said.

"Yes!" Mrs. Garcia said. "I'm impressed!"

"You've made a great discovery!" Mr. Garcia added.

Sam took the tooth in his hand and admired it. "It looks like it came from megalodon to me!" he said. "This tooth is probably worth several hundred dollars."

"NO!" squealed Evan. He snatched the tooth away and gingerly placed it in Mrs. Garcia's open palms. "It's PRICELESS!"

24

S'MORES & SNORES

Back at Palmetto Bluff, *The Mimi* docked under a full moon that glistened on the May River like a Fourth of July fireworks show. They had dropped off Mr. and Mrs. Garcia and Sam at the Bluffton town dock.

"Just leave all this junk—uh, I mean STEM stuff—in the boat," a weary Papa said. "We'll get it all in the morning."

The kids were worn out themselves—wet, muddy, and hungry. "I'm glad we decided to donate our tooth to The Conservancy," Avery said with a smile, as she climbed out of the boat. She held her hand out in the moonlight, trying to remind herself of just how big and beautiful that priceless tooth was. She almost hoped the little nick in her thumb wouldn't heal too fast, though she knew Mimi would soon cover it with antibacterial medicine and a big band-aid.

"Since lots of people will see it, does that make us famous?" Evan eagerly asked.

"Of course!" replied Noah.

"I'm too pooped to cook dinner," Mimi hinted, as Papa helped her out of the boat.

"That's why they call this the Poop Deck," Papa teased. "You can all stand here and hose off and clean up and we'll go to Canoe for dinner."

"I don't think I can eat on another boat today," Evan groaned, holding his queasy stomach.

"Canoe is the restaurant at the boathouse, Evan," Mimi reassured her grandson. She and Papa headed up the dock.

Avery, Evan, and Noah lagged behind. "We did good, didn't we?" Evan said.

"Well, if the adults knew all we did, they'd say we pushed the envelope of safety," Avery said with a giggle. "But I guess that's how you solve mysteries."

"Somebody's gotta solve 'em," said Noah, with a grin so big his teeth glowed in the moonlight. "It might as well be kids."

"Are you kids clean yet?" Papa bellowed from the top of the dock.

"From STEM...to stern!" Avery promised, shutting off the hose.

"Want some grilled cheese for dinner?" Avery teased Evan as they headed up the dock.

"NO!" said Evan. "All I want are, uh, is, uh," he thought and thought, walking slower, "are S'mores and snores!"

And that's what Mimi and Papa let him order for dinner, and after he'd eaten one, he fell sound asleep at the table.

The End

DO YOU LIKE MYSTERIES?

You have the chance to solve them!
You can solve little mysteries,
like figuring out
how to do your homework and
why your dog always hides your shoes.

You can solve big mysteries, like how to
program a fun computer game,
protect an endangered animal,
find a new energy source,
INVENT A NEW WAY TO DO SOMETHING,
explore outer space, and more!

You may be surprised to find
that *science*, **technology**,
engineering, math, and even
HISTORY, literature, and
ART can help you solve all kinds of
"mysteries" you encounter.

So feed your curiosity, learn all you can, apply
your creativity, and **be a mystery-solver too!**

– Carole Marsh

More about the Science, Technology,
Engineering, & Math in this book

THE ENGINEERING DESIGN PROCESS

Engineers follow a series of logical, thoughtful steps
in the process of solving a problem. Although some
problems may be more complicated than other problems,
the basic steps are the same!

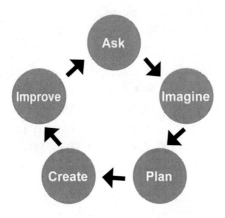

Ask! What is the problem? What have others done
about it?

Imagine! What are some solutions? Brainstorm ideas
and make your choice.

Plan! Visualize your plan in a diagram or chart, and
list the materials you will need.

Create! Follow your plan and test out your solution.

Improve! Decide what works and what doesn't, and
improve your design.

WHAT IS A POLYGON?

A polygon is a flat, closed shape with straight sides.

Polygons are named for the number of sides they have.

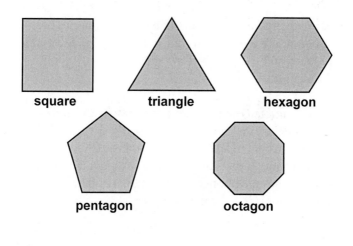

square   triangle   hexagon

pentagon   octagon

SHARK SIZES
LITTLE, BIG, AND MEGA-BIG

At 7 inches long, the dwarf lantern shark is the smallest shark.

The whale shark is the largest shark alive today. It can grow nearly 50 feet long!

The prehistoric megalodon shark may have been as large as 100 feet long!

HIGH TIDE, OR LOW TIDE?

Have you ever noticed how the ocean moves up and down throughout the day? At the beach, sometimes you have lots of sand to walk on, and at other times the water comes up high on the shore. In bays and estuaries near the ocean, the water drains out, exposing plant life and sandbars, and then the water comes back in, covering them up again.

This rise and fall of the ocean happens twice each day. These changes are known as tides. Tides are caused by the gravitational pull of the moon and the sun on the earth. Although the sun is much larger than the moon, the moon has the strongest gravitational pull because it is so much closer to the earth!

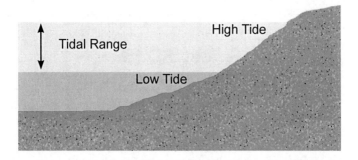

The intertidal area is the area of the ocean shore between the low-tide and high-tide lines. It is an always-changing habitat for uniquely-adapted plants and animals!

SHARK TEETH: NOT ALL ALIKE

Different types of sharks have different kinds of teeth. Why? They have different kinds of teeth so they can capture and hold onto a specific type of prey!

 Tooth with serrated edge for catching and tearing apart prey (great white shark, hammerhead shark, tiger shark)

Thin, knife-like tooth to catch slippery fish (lemon shark, mako shark)

 Thick, flat, or conical teeth to crush crabs and mollusks (nurse shark, angel shark)

Sharks have multiple rows of teeth—so when a tooth is lost, it is immediately replaced by another one! Sharks continuously make new teeth so they are always ready to replace the ones they lose.

SHARKS AT RISK

In Asia, shark fin soup is a delicacy and overfishing has led to the declining number of sharks. As many as 73 million sharks are killed each year just for their fins.

SONAR

Sonar is an acronym for *Sound Navigation And Ranging.*

Sonar is a system that uses sound waves to locate objects under water. Sonar works by sending out sound waves and then measuring how long it takes for the waves to be reflected and returned. This process can be used to find underwater objects such as submarines, rocks, fish, and shipwrecks. It can also be used to detect the depth of a body of water, and map the ocean floor.

Hammerhead sharks have a natural type of sonar. This sonar is known as **echolocation**. Scientists believe that hammerhead sharks use echolocation to find prey and avoid predators.

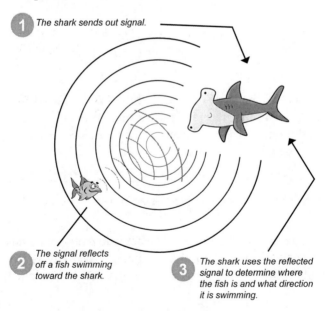

1 The shark sends out signal.

2 The signal reflects off a fish swimming toward the shark.

3 The shark uses the reflected signal to determine where the fish is and what direction it is swimming.

SHARK FACTS

- Sharks have a reputation for being the bully of the oceans, but only 20 of the more than 350 species of sharks have ever been known to attack humans.

- Sharks have been known to gobble garbage. Tires, license plates, and even gas tanks have been found in the stomachs of tiger sharks!

- Sharks can hear a fish thrashing in the water as far as 500 meters away.

- Like many animals, sharks use camouflage. The topsides of most sharks are dark to blend with the water above them and their undersides are light to blend in with the ocean floor.

- Talk about a great sniffer! Sharks can detect blood in the water from miles away!

- Sharks are like the airplanes of the ocean. Their tails create forward movement like an airplane's propeller. Water moves over their fins the way air moves over an airplane's wings!

- When sharks need to hunt in icy water, they can heat their eyes with special organs that are next to the muscles in their eye sockets.

- The organs on a shark's nose that sense electricity given off by other animals are called ampullae of Lorenzini.

- At one time, sailors referred to sharks as "sea dogs." Maybe that's why their babies are called "pups"!

- Before the invention of sandpaper, shark skin was used to polish wood!

GLOSSARY

animated – lively and energetic

cartilage – a strong, flexible material found in some parts of the body, such as the nose, outer ear, and some joints

coincidence – related events that seem to have been planned but weren't

commotion – a disturbance

endangered – exposed to peril or extinction

engineering – the process of applying scientific and mathematical knowledge to practical ends, such as the design and building of structures, engines, electrical equipment, etc.

expedition – an outing or journey taken for a specific purpose, often for discovery

fossil – the remains of a living thing from a former geologic age, found in earth or rock

habitat – the natural environment of a plant or animal

impractical – not sensible or realistic to do

latitude – distance north or south of the equator measured in degrees

limestone – a rock formed chiefly from animal remains (such as shells or coral) that is used for building and making cement

longitude – distance east or west of the prime meridian measured in degrees

marine biologist – a person who studies the living organisms that live in seas or oceans

mischievous – fond of tricks

paleontologist – a scientist who studies fossils to understand living things from former geologic periods

persistently – continuing to do something even though it is difficult

quarry – a large open hole or pit dug for mining stone, marble, gravel, etc.

sedimentary rock – rock made from layers of sediment that were carried and deposited by water, ice and wind

species – a variety, type, or kind of plant or animal

recede – to move back or away

serrated – having a jagged or saw-like edge

shoal – a sandbar or reef

skeptical – doubting what is seen or heard

unconventional – different from the norm

velocity – quickness of motion; speed

Enjoy this exciting excerpt from:

THE MYSTERY AT

ALLIGATOR ALLEY

1

GATOR BAIT

Evan watched bubbles gurgle up from the murky water. They skimmed across the dark surface, turning slowly to display rainbows of color, before popping unexpectedly. Frustrated, he lay down his fishing pole and stretched out on the spongy ground. Mashed potato clouds were piled high on a blue plate sky. Sure, the scenery was beautiful at the Savannah National Wildlife Refuge, but Evan was disappointed. He'd been here with his cousin Christina and his sister Avery for several hours, and he hadn't even caught a fish. He had seen plenty of wildlife—wood storks, deer, ducks, and all sorts of critters, except the one he wanted to see most—an **alligator.**

Evan closed his eyes and let his imagination run wild as a wildebeest. He was holding a glistening knife between his teeth and glaring bravely into the eyes of the prehistoric-looking beast. Always the hero, he warned his sister and cousin to stay back and dove onto the scaly back of an alligator more than twice his size! The gator plunged into the water, taking Evan with him. He rolled over and over like a log. Evan was about to get the best of the **cantankerous** creature when something interrupted his daydream.

His eyes snapped open. Something had really chomped down on his earlobe! Evan jumped to his feet and flailed his arms wildly. "Help!" he screamed. "A gator's got me!"

Startled, Christina and Avery looked up from their sketchpads. Both were busy drawing a tall sandhill crane wading near the bank. Evan's commotion scared the lanky bird. It sounded like a bugler warning the other wildlife of danger before its large gray wings lifted it into the air.

Fearing her little brother was being gobbled alive, Avery slung her pad and pencil. They splashed in the water's edge. Christina jumped to her feet, ready to help her cousin fight off his vicious foe, but instead started laughing. Dangling from Evan's ear like a pirate's earring was a little green lizard.

Christina gently plucked the wriggling fellow from his ear like she was picking a pepper from a plant and placed it gently on the ground. "You gotta watch out for those gators," she said, winking at her cousin.

Evan held one hand over his pounding heart and rubbed his earlobe with the other. He quickly checked his fingers to make sure there was no blood.

"Not even a scratch," Avery said, examining her brother's ear. "The little guy probably thought you were a juicy worm lying in the grass. He only pinched you. He doesn't even have any teeth!"

Evan shuddered. "If that was a pinch, I'd hate to see what a real gator could do!"

"I hope you never get close enough to find out!" Christina said. "Alligators are serious business. You should never get anywhere near them."

Christina couldn't believe her own ears. She sounded just like her grandparents. For years, she'd gotten herself and her brother Grant into plenty of **predicaments**. They'd followed their mystery-writing grandmother Mimi and their cowboy-pilot grandfather Papa all over the world. But now she was a college student at the Savannah College of

Art and Design in nearby Savannah, Georgia. Her "what they don't know won't hurt them" attitude was gone.

She remembered it was a gator encounter that had brought her here in the first place. Mimi and Papa, who'd recently moved to Palmetto Bluff, South Carolina, had already planned to have their grandkids at their new home when the accident happened. Mimi was playing a round of golf at the May River Golf Club when her ball rolled into a small pond. When she reached in to get it, she found herself ankle to eye with a small gator.

"I walked on air!" Mimi had told them. But when she came down, the impact broke her leg. Now she was home, miserable, and Papa was taking care of her. They were unable to do all the things they'd planned during the grandkids' fall school break, including taking Avery and Evan to the wildlife **refuge**. Christina was proud she could fill in, at least for the day.

KERSPLASH! The sound came from where Christina and Avery had been practicing their art. Avery saw that her sketchpad was now back on the bank. She walked over and picked up the soggy paper. *Something had taken a big bite out of it!*